THE BANANA BUNCH

For Sheila, without whom these stories would never have been written.

THE BANANA BUNCH

Written by Dawn Carroll

Illustrated by Linden Hare

SUNNYDAYS PUBLISHING

Copyright © Dawn Carroll 2012
Illustrations © Linden Hare 2012
First published in 2012 by Sunnydays Publishing
c/o Amolibros, Loundshay Manor Cottage, Preston Bowyer, Milverton, Somerset TA4 1QF

Distributed by Gardners Books, 1 Whittle Drive, Eastbourne, East Sussex, BN23 6QH
Tel: +44(0)1323 521555 | Fax: +44(0)1323 521666

www.amolibros.com

British Library Cataloguing in Publication Data
A catalogue record for this book is available from the British Library.

ISBN 978-0-9567447-0-8

Typeset by Amolibros, Milverton, Somerset
This book production has been managed by Amolibros
Printed and bound by the Lavenham Press, Lavenham, Suffolk, UK

FOREWORD

Being asked to write the foreword for this book is a real privilege. These heart-warming stories about the mischievous adventures of a family of monkeys and their covert endeavours are enhanced by incredibly delightful illustrations by Linden Hare, which both my three young children and I thoroughly enjoyed.

As a parent, Winston's Wish and Tŷ Hafan charities are very close to my heart as they offer so much valuable support and comfort to so many young people.

These stories, affectionately dedicated to a dear friend in hospital, have left me feeling truly inspired. Dawn's initial "one-off" card to cheer her friend Sheila has, through a huge collective effort, been published for many others to share and enjoy.

Stephen Terry, The Hardwick

STICKY BANANA AND DATE LOAF

A perfect recipe for bananas, Stephen felt the book would not be complete without dedicating this to the monkeys!

1pt	Boiling water	2oz	Dark brown sugar
10oz	Chopped bananas	2	Eggs
5oz	Chopped dates	1lb	Flour
4oz	Soft brown sugar	2tsp	Baking powder
6oz	Caster sugar	2tsp	Bicarbonate of soda
4oz	Butter		

1. Line a 30cm x 20cm x 4cm tin with baking paper and pre-heat oven at 150°C.
2. In one bowl, cream butter and sugar.
3. In a separate bowl add chopped bananas and dates and mix with flour, bicarbonate, and baking powder.
4. Whisk the 2 eggs then slowly add them to the butter and sugar mixture.
5. Blend the two mixtures together and slowly stir in the boiling water.
6. Pour the mixture into the tin and bake for approximately 2 hours.

INTRODUCTION

The original monkey stories were written in 2007 when Sheila, a family friend, suddenly became unwell.

Until the onset of her illness Sheila was the epitome of robust good health – ebullient, outgoing and generous with her time and talents on behalf of others. She also had a luminous smile, a wicked sense of humour and a highly infectious laugh.

It was a great shock to hear of Sheila's illness. "Get Well Soon" cards were immediately sent by the author and her family.

Very soon they learned that Sheila hated the hospital food. The fact that both Sheila and the author shared their homes with a number of furry, soft toy monkeys then provided the inspiration for a series of home-made "monkey" cards.

The original cards consisted of photographs, combined with the adventures of the monkeys as they tried to deliver bananas to the hospital. Sheila loved the cards and it was her wish that they should be published.

The stories in this book are not quite the same as those that were written for the original cards – which remain with Sheila's family. The illustrations are also entirely new.

The author could not have created Sheila's cards on her own and owes huge thanks to her family, friends and neighbours who, once they understood the nature of the project, came up with countless ideas for story lines and an amazing assortment of clothing and props for the original photos.

Thanks are also due to the strangers who gave of their time and enthusiasm when presented with apparently mad requests for the temporary loan of their fire engine, lorry and ladder so that photos of large, furry, monkeys could be taken for the original cards.

The author is also utterly indebted to Linden who has given untold hours of her own time to produce illustrations that totally capture the spirit of the stories originally written for Sheila, and the good nature of the monkeys. This book could not have been produced without her help.

The kindness and generosity of all who have contributed to the creation of Sheila's cards, and the book, have been exceptional.

Profits from the sale of the first edition of this book will be donated to Winston's Wish and Tŷ Hafan

A full list of acknowledgements can be found at the back of the book.

MONTAGUE FAMILY TREE

Millicent m **Merlin**
Merrifield Montague

Matthew m Melissa
Montague Moreton

Marianna m **Matthias**
Marchmont Montague

Marcellus m Maria
Montague Moncrief

Martha m Mallory
Montague Mackenzie

Montgomery m Marigold
Montague McCreavey

Melisande m Martyn
Montague Meadowsweet

Morgan m Magnolia
(Bruiser) Merryweather
Montague

Mathilda m **Michel**
Montague Le Singe

Marshall Montana
Mackenzie Mackenzie

Myrtle Marguerite
Meadowsweet Meadowsweet

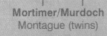

Sophie Sebastian Marcel
Le Singe Le Singe Le Singe

Montague Maximillian Montmorency Minerva Moriarty/Mycroft
Montague Montague Montague Montague Montague (twins)

Monty Mortimer/Murdoch Miranda Martyn
Montague Montague (twins) Montague Montague

Saturday 3rd March

Hello Granny Millicent. Oh my golly gosh and goodness! I can hardly wait to tell you what we have been doing today.

It all started when our human friend Sheila telephoned to tell us that she is in hospital at the moment. Sheila is normally such a cheerful lady, but she is ever so grumpy about the hospital food. Apparently it is awful!

We, of course, recommended that Sheila should eat plenty of health-giving bananas and were shocked when she told us that there are no bananas on the food menu at our local hospital. No bananas available in a hospital?! It is a national disgrace. Surely everyone knows that bananas are essential for maintenance of good health and shiny fur?

1

For a few moments we were too amazed to know what to say or do but then Montgomery had one of his brilliant ideas.

I do wish you and Grandpa Merlin could have been here this morning when we gathered together to raise large glasses of banana milkshake to celebrate the formation of The Banana Bunch – a new and secret society which is dedicated to the delivery of best quality, fresh bananas to as many unwell people as possible.

The children are positively bubbling with enthusiasm and Montgomery has already been down to Bristol Docks where he has purchased several large crates of highest quality, organic, fair-trade bananas (delicious!). We plan to deliver the first batch of bananas to Sheila and all the other hungry people at our local hospital this very afternoon.

By the way, thank you for your last letter. Australia sounds marvellous. We were, though, all a little concerned to hear that Grandpa Merlin's paw was bitten while he was trying to feed a koala bear at the zoo. How clever of you to use a spare banana skin when you couldn't find a bandage.

Lots of love, Marigold

PS I'll write again this evening when we get back from delivering bananas to the hospital. It is all so exciting!

TREETOP COTTAGE
FOREST OF DEAN

Saturday 3rd March

Dear Granny Millicent,

Well, honestly! I am so distressed by the events of this afternoon that my paws are still shaking.

We were positive that we would be made welcome when we arrived at our local hospital this afternoon, full of smiles and enthusiasm and carrying bunches of the very best quality bananas.

Instead, we had barely set paws inside the building when people started shouting, "No monkeys allowed," and a lot of other things that I cannot possibly write down. We were thoroughly shocked.

Since getting home we have discussed the situation and the whole family is in agreement. We will not be deterred from our banana delivery work. If The Banana Bunch cannot deliver bananas openly we will do it by stealth!

By good fortune the youngster's cousins Sophie, Sebastian and Marcel le Singe have just arrived from France for a long visit. Marcel (who says he has always wanted to learn to fly an aeroplane) has bravely volunteered to lead our first banana delivery mission.

Marcel has borrowed a "How to Fly in 6 Easy Lessons" instruction manual from the local library and is studying the contents keenly. We expect to be ready to make the first delivery of bananas in just a few days from now.

I will write again just as soon as we have air-dropped the bananas into the hospital.

Loads of love, Marigold

TREETOP COTTAGE
FOREST OF DEAN

Wednesday 7th March

Dear Granny Millicent,

I am most awfully sorry to have to tell you that our attempt at dropping bananas by aeroplane didn't quite go to plan.

It was certainly not Marcel's fault. He flew the aeroplane beautifully. The trouble was that the boxes didn't cope too well with landing on the tarmac at the front entrance of the hospital. Quite a few passers-by slid on the scattered and squashed bananas.

It was all most upsetting. We had been so certain that the people on the ground would be delighted to see the bananas arrive. Instead they all

seemed to be shouting and waving their fists at our aeroplane.

We could not hear their words because of the noise of the aeroplane engine but we do hope that they were not saying anything impolite. Bad words make our fur stand on end!

We do, of course, feel awfully guilty about the people who fell over but we are still determined to deliver those health-giving bananas. We have an alternative plan.

Next time our brave volunteers Montmorency and Minerva are going to parachute into the hospital, carrying large rucksacks full of bananas on their backs. We are certain that this will be the best way to ensure that the bananas arrive in perfect condition and can see no possible way in which this plan can go wrong.

Minerva is thoroughly enjoying the parachute training classes but Montmorency doesn't seem quite so keen. Never mind. The Banana Bunch never give up. Our intrepid duo will be setting off to deliver some bananas just as soon as Montmorency has conquered his fear of heights.

Lots of love from Marigold

TREETOP COTTAGE
FOREST OF DEAN

Friday 9th March

Dear Granny Millicent,

Oh dear. I'm afraid that yet another small problem has struck our banana delivery plan.

I was so proud as I watched Montmorency and Minerva jumping out of the aeroplane with their rucksacks of bananas. In fact, I was so convinced that they were going to succeed that I was in the middle of telephoning the good news to our friend Sheila. And then, at the very last minute, a gust of wind blew the gallant parachutists off course – such a shame.

The people who raced out from the nearby hospital building made a terrible fuss. Poor Montmorency and Minerva were tangled up in a horrid heap of parachute fabric and bananas but no one tried to help them. Instead they just kept shouting that two monkeys had landed on top of the car belonging to someone important at the hospital.

Such discourtesy. From all the noise anyone would have thought that Montmorency and Minerva had intended to create those monkey-shaped dents in the roof of the car!

And worse was to follow. My fur positively stood on end when I learned that Montmorency and Minerva had been whisked away to jail.

We are, of course, very embarrassed that such young members of the Montague family will soon have a criminal record.

The Banana Bunch have, however, vowed to deliver bananas and we must do whatever is necessary. With this in mind I have baked an extra large banana cake and have hidden a map, compass and hacksaw inside it, just in case they need to escape!

Lots of love, Marigold

TREETOP COTTAGE
FOREST OF DEAN

Saturday 10th March

Dear Granny Millicent,

I do hope that you are still having fun in Australia. Do please send love to Melisande, Martyn and nieces Myrtle and Marguerite. It was so nice to hear that young Myrtle will be returning to the UK with you. We are all very much looking forward to meeting her.

I am sure that you will be relieved to hear that Montmorency and Minerva were released from jail yesterday. I suspect that they would have been allowed to come home sooner if they had been able to explain why they were parachuting into the hospital but, being very honourable monkeys, they kept the secret of The Banana Bunch. We are so proud of them.

Their adventure has, though, been rather useful.

While sitting in their prison cells Montmorency and Minerva remembered seeing films about prisoners who dug tunnels to get out of jail. And so they came up with the positively brilliant idea that, if prisoners can tunnel out of jail, surely we can tunnel into a hospital. They are such clever monkeys.

Montague and his French cousin, Sebastian, have volunteered for this exciting mission. They have borrowed a book about the history of coal mining from the local library and are now gathering together the necessary pickaxes, helmets and Miner's Lamps.

The heroic twosome will be setting out just as soon as they have worked out how to light the lamps.

Lots of love, Marigold

PS Apparently a canary would be helpful. We don't suppose you can think of anyone in the family who could lend one to us for a day or so?

TREETOP COTTAGE
FOREST OF DEAN

Wednesday 14th March

Dear Granny Millicent,

Thank you so much for your letter. We thoroughly enjoyed hearing about the day when you and Grandpa went surfing at Bondi Beach. It sounds very exciting. Did it take a very long time for your fur to dry out afterwards?

Back here in the UK I'm afraid that things haven't been going quite so well.

It is really most embarrassing but we honestly don't know how our latest banana delivery mission is progressing. We have not heard anything from Montague and Sebastian since they set off to tunnel into the local hospital several days ago.

Of course we are not worried about Montague and Sebastian. They are such wise and clever monkeys that we are certain that they are OK. We are, though, all becoming rather concerned that they may have felt the need to eat some of the bananas en route to sustain them during their tunnelling work. We fear that very few bananas may remain uneaten by now!

In the face of such uncertainty my dearest Montgomery has done something rather foolish.

While searching in the attic Montgomery found a large fireworks rocket that was left over from last year's Guy Fawkes' night party.

I and the children did try to tell him that using a rocket to transport both him and a rucksack of bananas to the hospital would be a bad idea, but would he listen?

He is now temporarily absent from home receiving treatment for burns which are in some rather embarrassing places…

It seems very quiet here without Montgomery but I am sure that he will be home soon, full of bright ideas for new banana delivery techniques. In the meantime we are all busily discussing the problem at our daily Banana Bunch meetings.

I will send news just as soon as we hear from Montague and Sebastian.

Loads of love, Marigold

TREETOP COTTAGE
FOREST OF DEAN

Saturday 17th March

Dear Granny Millicent,

It is such a relief to be able to tell you that Montague and Sebastian returned home several days ago. Distressingly I also have to tell you that their mission did not go smoothly.

Tunnelling proved to be harder work than they had expected. By the time our heroes finally reached home they were covered in mud and totally exhausted.

We were all terribly sympathetic when they apologised for eating the entire crate of bananas. Digging must be such very hungry work.

We were, though, delighted to hear that they had successfully tunnelled almost as far as the main hospital corridor and we thoroughly approved their plan of returning today, to complete the tunnel.

I am sure you will share my distress when I tell you what happened next.

Just as Montague and Sebastian were about to set off this morning, carrying pickaxes, lamps and a new box of best bananas, we heard a local radio news report.

It seems that a large hole in the ground, full of old banana skins, suddenly opened up near the main entrance of the local hospital last night. The authorities are now apparently seeking the "vandals" who have been digging beneath the hospital foundations.

We were shocked by the news and very briefly wondered if Montague and Sebastian might have been responsible. We rapidly dismissed this silly idea.

Montague and Sebastian could not possibly have been to blame. They studied their *Mining History* library book very thoroughly indeed.

The presence of banana skins in the hole is, though, a little puzzling. We

are beginning to wonder whether a rival branch of The Banana Bunch might have been at work?

Lots of love from Marigold

TREETOP COTTAGE
FOREST OF DEAN

Wednesday 21st March

Dear Granny Millicent,

Gosh, what an exciting time you are having during your world tour. We are all very much looking forward to seeing the video of you, Grandpa and Myrtle zooming down the rapids during your white-water rafting trip in New Zealand. It must have been such fun when your boat capsized and you all fell into the water!

I am delighted to be able to tell you that Montgomery has returned from the Burns Hospital. We hope that he will soon be able to sit down more comfortably, though he is still awfully embarrassed about the lack of fur on his posterior.

Unfortunately, in his enthusiasm to make up for the failure of his recent rocket banana delivery attempt he was rather impulsive.

It all came about because he has had to borrow a long coat to cover up his bald patches while his fur re-grows.

As soon as Montgomery saw the coat he decided that it would be the perfect cover for smuggling several large bunches of bananas into the local hospital.

And even when we warned him that he would be recognised as the monkey whose rocket had set the hospital roof on fire last week he remained determined. He assured us that he would be wearing the perfect disguise.

Oh dear, Oh dear. The disguise turned out to be the long coat together with a pair of very dark sunglasses.

The first I knew of the disaster was when I heard the sound of one large monkey and many bananas rattling down the front steps of the house. Montgomery had only made it as far as the front door before the combination of the long coat hem and being unable to see through his dark glasses resulted in an extremely messy fall.

He is currently in the bathroom, washing off several pounds of squashed bananas.

Such a shame. They were awfully good bananas.

Ah well, it is only a temporary setback. The children have another plan.

Heaps of love, Marigold

TREETOP COTTAGE
FOREST OF DEAN

Saturday 24th March

Dear Granny Millicent,

Thank you so much for your kind enquiries about Montgomery's fur. It is almost back to normal. In fact, he and the children are already preparing for the next banana delivery attempt.

Montgomery was keen to do the job on his own but, after a family conference, we decided that it would probably be wiser to make this a team effort…

We don't want to hurt Montgomery's feelings. My darling husband is, as you well know, one of the most intelligent of monkeys. He can, though, be just

the tiniest bit absent-minded and things do rather seem to go wrong when he sets off on his own!

In the nick of time (just as Montgomery was thinking of trying the rocket idea again) Minerva found a marvellous book and I am certain that we now have the ideal plan for banana delivery.

Of course, it is a little unhelpful that the book came from a second-hand shop and that quite a few of the pages seem to be missing...

As you can see from the enclosed photograph the team are currently having a little difficulty persuading the carpet to move.

I don't suppose you might know the words that are used to make a magic carpet fly?...

Lots of love, Marigold

TREETOP COTTAGE
FOREST OF DEAN

Sunday 25th March

Dear Granny Millicent,

I am most awfully sorry to have to tell you that the magic carpet proved a little more troublesome than we had expected.

With great skill Marcel (you will remember that he flew our aeroplane) managed to persuade the carpet to take off for a test run. At first, everyone seemed to be having tremendous fun as the carpet zoomed vertically upwards at a positively exhilarating speed.

Shortly after this Marcel shouted down that he couldn't find the steering wheel.

I'm sure you can imagine my feelings as I watched them all tumble to the ground when the carpet made a particularly sharp turn in mid-air.

I am sending you a photograph of the wounded heroes. They have all asked me to tell you that falling off was really quite good fun, and that they don't mind their injuries at all.

They do, though, feel dreadfully bad that most of them landed on top of Sebastian who had remained on the ground to guard the banana supply during the test flight. Thankfully Sebastian was only slightly squashed. The bananas, though, suffered rather badly.

Any further banana delivery attempts are clearly out of the question for the next week or so, but never fear.

I have been in touch with our monkey relatives in Wales and they are keen to set up a Welsh branch of The Banana Bunch. They have offered to take over banana delivery duty until the English team have recovered.

Lots of love, Marigold

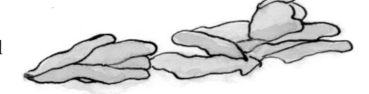

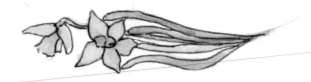

THE DAFFODIL HOUSE
SUGARLOAF MOUNTAIN

Wednesday 28th March

Dear Grandma Millicent,

Thank you so much for all of your letters. Your trip to Fiji sounds brilliant. I can hardly wait to see the photos of Grandpa Merlin para-sailing behind the boat.

Has Marigold told you that we have been asked to take over the duties of the English branch of The Banana Bunch temporarily? We are so pleased to be able to help. And, while I wouldn't dream of criticising Marigold and her family, I did have to laugh when I heard that they had tried to use a second-hand magic carpet!

35

Now that the Welsh branch of The Banana Bunch are in charge I can positively guarantee that Sheila's long-delayed bananas will finally be delivered.

Our plan is very simple. We have arranged to borrow a helicopter from our friends at the SMS (that's the Special Monkey Squadron, just in case you didn't know).

Luckily for us, Murdoch gained his Pilot's Licence several years ago by means of a correspondence course. He is absolutely confident that he will be able to keep the helicopter hovering over the roof of the hospital while Mortimer and Miranda abseil down ropes with rucksacks full of best quality bananas. Bruiser is so excited at the prospect of being the navigator.

The moment the folks at the hospital hear the rotor blades the first delivery of health-giving bananas will be only minutes away.

Positively foolproof.

I will write tomorrow to tell you of our success.

Love and hugs, Magnolia and the family

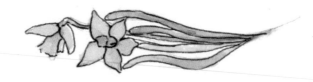

THE DAFFODIL HOUSE
SUGARLOAF MOUNTAIN

Thursday 29th March

Dear Grandma Millicent,

It pains me to have to tell you that things did not go entirely to plan. I am beginning to suspect that this secret banana delivery lark is more complicated than it seems at first glance.

Much to his surprise Murdoch found the helicopter controls the teensiest bit challenging. It seems that helicopters were not covered during his correspondence course.

Everyone on board was a little surprised too. They had not realised that a helicopter could fly upside down.

But things were getting better and Murdoch undoubtedly would have got the hang of the controls if the helicopter had not run into that inconveniently placed radio mast.

After that things went from bad to worse.

I am quite sure that the SMS must have a few spare helicopter rotor blades lying around somewhere, and will be able to fix the helicopter with no difficulty at all, but they are making a most unreasonable fuss about Murdoch's little accident.

I am sure you will be as shocked as I was to hear that my darling husband Bruiser, together with Murdoch, Mortimer and Miranda have all been sent to jail. Outrageous!

But never fear. We Welsh monkeys are extremely resourceful. I confidently predict that they will all be home soon.

In the meantime, while they are away, I am working on a new plan...

Love and hugs, Magnolia

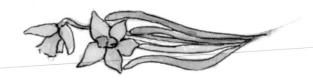

THE DAFFODIL HOUSE
SUGARLOAF MOUNTAIN

Friday 30th March

Dear Grandma Millicent,

The good news is that Bruiser and the rest of the helicopter team have come home.

The bad news is that they were so alarmed at being told that they were going to be locked up for several weeks that they panicked and broke out of jail.

It seems that a group of visitors arrived at the jail, very shortly after Bruiser, Mortimer, Murdoch and Miranda were placed there. It being such a hot day, most of the visitors very soon took off their hats and jackets.

A helpful Prison Officer then hung the hats and jackets on hooks very close to the cell doors – obviously not realising that monkeys have extremely long arms.

Quick as a flash Bruiser had "borrowed" the clothing and Murdoch had started work on picking the locks of the cell doors using the pin attached to Miranda's brooch. I was shocked to discover that he has learned to do this from watching films.

Once outside the cell they found that their new clothing worked wonders. They apparently only had to approach a door for the person standing nearby to give them a big salute and open the door. They were all rather puzzled by this, but also very grateful and, very soon, they were all outside the jail.

Oh dear, Oh dear. I am sure they would have been released anyway if they had waited for just a little while longer – and had explained the importance of their banana delivery mission. But being such honourable monkeys they did not want to break the Banana Bunch vow of secrecy, and they are now all "wanted" criminals.

I simply cannot imagine what will happen next. It is all so unfair. They were only trying to be good, kind monkeys.

Of course, this does not mean that we have given up on our banana delivery mission. The valiant escapees, Bruiser, Monty, Murdoch and Miranda, are at this very moment on their way to the greengrocery shop to collect a large bag of best bananas.

Do please wish us luck.

With lots of love from a very anxious Magnolia

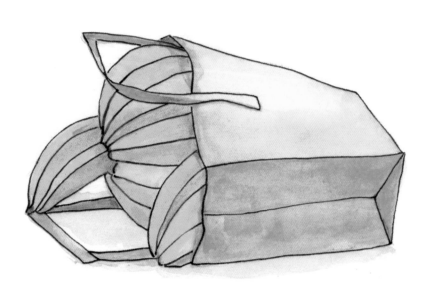

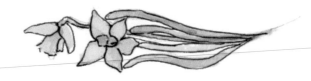

THE DAFFODIL HOUSE
SUGARLOAF MOUNTAIN

Sunday 1st April

Dear Great Grandma Milly

Gosh, I did like your latest letter. Antarctica sounds so exciting. We all laughed aloud at the description of your whale-watching boat going up and down and all over the place in the heavy sea. What a shame that you were all seasick and had to spend the whole of the trip in your cabin.

Things have also been a little difficult back here. You may remember that, after our escape from jail, we headed straight for the greengrocery shop.

And all seemed to be going well until we arrived at the shop – when we heard a loud voice say, "It's them. They're wanted."

When I first heard these words I got a nice warm, cuddly feeling inside, thinking how nice it was to be wanted and cared for.

But then we discovered that we were "wanted" in quite a different way!

It seems that the people from whom we borrowed the clothing that helped us to escape from jail are very cross with us and want their clothes back.

Fortunately there was just enough time for us to run off to hide in the nearby shrubbery. I had a lovely time drawing a picture of everyone while we waited.

With big hugs from Miranda

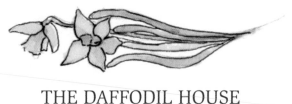

THE DAFFODIL HOUSE
SUGARLOAF MOUNTAIN

Sunday 1st April

Dear Grandma Millicent,

I really do wish that I could send good news about the family's latest banana delivery attempt but alas...

After sitting under a rather damp hedge for several hours, Bruiser, Monty, Murdoch and Miranda realised that the only way to get past the chap who was guarding the greengrocer's shop would be to adopt a disguise. They immediately sneaked away to a local shop from which one can hire fancy dress costumes and wigs.

Their disguises were so good that even I didn't recognise them when they reached home an hour or so ago. It is just such a shame that the rest of their brilliant plan failed.

Having purchased a large supply of extra high quality bananas Bruiser and the children (who had chosen athletic kit and long wigs as their disguise) jogged to the hospital and sneaked in – intending to deliver the bananas by paw.

Unfortunately Monty's baseball cap slid off at the crucial moment and a cry of "There's a monkey in the ward" went up. Our valiant heroes had to run away very fast and they suddenly found themselves in an empty room on the floor above the Childrens' Ward.

Being such clever and determined monkeys they immediately came up with an alternative plan, and it seemed such a good one at the time.

The idea was that Murdoch and Miranda would hold onto Bruiser's feet while he dangled out of a window. Bruiser then intended to drop the bananas through the open window of the ward below.

We now know that Bruiser has rather ticklish feet…

We are just hopeful that the children and nurses were not too confused or upset by the sight of five kilos of prime bananas and a large monkey hurtling past their ward window.

Love and hugs, Magnolia

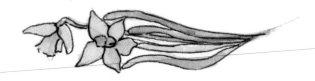

THE DAFFODIL HOUSE
SUGARLOAF MOUNTAIN

Monday 2nd April

Dear Grandma Millicent,

My goodness. You do seem to be having an exciting time in South America.
How very fortunate that it was only Myrtle's fur that was eaten by the
piranha fish when she dangled her paws into the water as your canoe
travelled up the Amazon river. Please reassure her that no one will laugh at
her patchy toes when she arrives to visit us.

I'm afraid that I also have some alarming news.

After the failure of their latest banana delivery attempt Bruiser, Monty,
Murdoch and Miranda were making their way home in search of consoling

afternoon tea and banana sandwiches when they spotted a chap who was putting up posters on all of the lamp posts.

When they looked at the posters they were appalled. The posters all showed Bruiser's handsome face!

It seems that the folks from whom Bruiser and the youngsters borrowed clothing, during their escape from jail, are still grumpy about the loss of their hats and jackets.

This most unfortunate turn of events means that Bruiser (and probably the rest of the family too) cannot take part in any more banana delivery attempts at the moment.

I have just spoken with Marigold. It was so embarrassing to have to explain that the Welsh branch of The Banana Bunch has also run into one or two teensy little problems but she was awfully nice about it. We have agreed that the English monkeys, who have now recovered from their flying carpet accident, will deliver Sheila's bananas as soon as possible.

Love and hugs from Magnolia and the family

TREETOP COTTAGE
FOREST OF DEAN

Wednesday 4th April

Dear Granny Millicent,

It was lovely to hear your news about your trip to Mexico. Second cousin Miguel Montagueros sounds such a nice chap. And the super-hot banana chilli casserole sounds absolutely amazing. Has Grandpa got his voice back yet?

As you probably know by now the Welsh branch of the family have had a spot of bad luck while trying to do the work of The Banana Bunch.

Never mind. The A Team are now back in charge and we are absolutely

confident that we will be able to send good news very soon. We have such a perfect new plan.

Moriarty and Mycroft are, of course, too young to actually take part in a banana delivery mission but they did come up with the latest idea.

Several days ago the twins were watching an American film in which a delivery boy rode on his bicycle past houses, flinging newspapers expertly onto doorsteps as he passed by. The moment they told us about this we all realised that they had come up with the perfect plan.

At the moment we are having a little difficulty with the bananas, which keep exploding as they hit the ground, but we are certain that we will be able to resolve this minor problem.

Just as soon as Montgomery and Montague have the technique perfected they will set off for the hospital and will whizz bunches of bananas through all the open windows. It is a method that simply cannot fail.

With lots of love from Marigold

TREETOP COTTAGE
FOREST OF DEAN

Saturday 7th April

Dear Granny Millicent,

Oh dear. Oh dear.

It was such a nice day when Montgomery and Montague set off to do their banana throwing practice that they decided to pop over the Severn Bridge for an enjoyable little zoom around the beautiful Welsh country lanes. It was a dreadful mistake.

No sooner had Montgomery brought the motorbike to a halt at the bridge toll booth than dozens of people started running towards him shouting, "It's him!"

Montgomery was so surprised that he simply didn't think of running away.

The good news is that Montague managed to escape with some bananas, though quite a lot of them did become rather bruised when he threw them at the people who were chasing him!

Meanwhile the whole family is in a state of shock that Montgomery has been taken to jail, having apparently been mistaken for his brother, Bruiser. Even worse, the story has appeared on the front page of this evening's local newspaper.

It is all quite outrageous. Montgomery is an innocent monkey!

With lots of love from a very worried Marigold

TREETOP COTTAGE
FOREST OF DEAN

Monday 9th April

Dear Granny Millicent,

I cannot tell you how relieved we all are. Montgomery was released from jail yesterday – but it was very much touch and go for quite a while.

It seems that the trouble with having fur between the toes is that the pawprints in the National Computer Pawprint Database all look pretty fuzzy. Fortunately, when Bruiser was arrested and paw-printed after the helicopter incident, he had a verruca.

After my poor Montgomery's pristine paws had been examined several times it was eventually agreed that he was not the wanted monkey.

Needless to say, this has all been most a most unpleasant experience. Montgomery has now gone away to spend a quiet week with his cousin Mackenzie Montague who has a house on a remote Scottish island. We very much hope that a week or so of best quality banana porridge and banana griddle cakes will help Montgomery to recover from the shock of his imprisonment.

Sophie, Montague, Maximillian, Marcel, Montmorency and Sebastian are also away from home at the moment, attending training courses for various occupations that may prove useful for future banana delivery missions.

I am enclosing a photograph of Sophie on the day when she won her rosette for being the best student in her "How to be a Florist" class.

It seems awfully quiet here at the moment with just Minerva and the twins at home, but it has been nice to rest my paws for a while.

The silence has also given Minerva and I time to think. We have come up with a new plan...

Lots of love, Marigold

TREETOP COTTAGE
FOREST OF DEAN

Tuesday 10th April

Dear Granny Millicent,

We are so excited. Minerva and I have finally managed to deliver some bananas to Sheila and all the other people at the hospital! I can't wait to tell Magnolia and all the other Welsh monkeys!

Montgomery might be a little cross with me as he did not wish us to do anything risky in his absence but we could not possibly delay delivery of those much needed bananas any longer.

We found some lovely outfits at our local charity shop, the hats of which hid our furry ears perfectly, and we set off this afternoon with two large shopping trolleys full of goodies.

Our disguises worked brilliantly and we have just returned from a very happy two hours distributing fresh bananas and banana cakes at the hospital. It was so nice to see so many people enjoying themselves.

We did have one big surprise, though. One lady refused our gifts and told us that she doesn't like bananas. Doesn't like bananas?! That is impossible. Everybody loves bananas!

We were so shocked that our fur stood on end. We came home looking more like hedgehogs than monkeys!

Having consumed several large glasses of banana milkshake and a good helping of banana fritters we are now much calmer and have started to feel sorry for the lady. Clearly she has never experienced proper banana cuisine.

Having spent the last hour looking through recipe books in search of a tempting dish I have decided to cook one of Montgomery's favourite snacks for her – banana and pickled onion cheesecake. Surely no one could dislike that?

Loads of love, Marigold

TREETOP COTTAGE
FOREST OF DEAN

Monday 16th April

Dear Granny Millicent,

Oh dear. Oh dear. After our previous success we were absolutely certain that everything would go well today. I had even spent the whole weekend baking special banana pasties and biscuits to be taken to the hospital.

And it did go well for a while. We once again put on our disguises and were about to walk through the main doorway to the hospital when we saw a large poster. It stated "Visitors Must Remove Hats Before Entering The Hospital".

We were very upset but we also knew that the moment we took off our hats our furry ears would be seen and we would be recognised as monkeys.

With great sadness we turned around and came home – munching a few consoling banana biscuits as we walked.

But, as you know, a monkey never gives up and we have a splendid new plan.

We are pretty sure that even the folks at the hospital will not expect a smartly dressed official fire-fighter to remove his hat. And so, Montgomery has enrolled with the local Fire Service for a training course. His uniform should provide the perfect disguise for future banana deliveries.

He should graduate from the course within a week or two. At least, we hope so. The fire-fighting course seems to be just the tiniest bit strenuous and Montgomery is eating an awful lot of extra bananas to keep up his strength.

Never mind, we are very proud of him and we do still have a few bananas left for supper.

Masses of love, Marigold

TREETOP COTTAGE
FOREST OF DEAN

Sunday 22nd April

Dear Granny Millicent,

Gosh. We did enjoy reading your tale of the day when you all went scuba diving in the Caribbean Sea. Did it take a very long time to disentangle the jellyfish from Grandpa's fur?

I am pleased, and also very relieved, to be able to tell you that Montgomery has nearly finished his fire-fighting training course.

It seems that a monkey needs very strong muscles to make the fire hose point in the right direction. And as for all the running up and down ladders that his trainers insist upon...

Our noble Montgomery is positively ravenous when he gets home each evening. He has now has eaten so many extra bananas that there are none left at our local shops!

But, never fear. Maximillian has borrowed a motorbike and side-car and has just set off for Bristol Docks to collect lots of bananas, fresh from the ship.

Look out for my next letter. I predict that it will be bursting with news about how Montgomery has successfully delivered bananas to Sheila and the other patients at our local hospital while wearing his fire-fighter's uniform.

Loads of love, Marigold

TREETOP COTTAGE
FOREST OF DEAN

Thursday 26th April

Dearest Magnolia,

Oh gosh and golly. What an exciting day we have had. I am writing to let you know that the story is going to be in all the national newspapers!

As you know, we have found it a little tricky to actually get inside our local hospital. So we were delighted when Moriarty and Mycroft (who had been roller-skating near to the hospital) told us that lots of the downstairs windows are open at the moment because of the sunny weather.

We immediately realised that we could easily pop a crate or two of bananas through one of the open windows and we set off.

What happened next was all most unfortunate. Though perhaps it was a good thing that we found the spiders first, when we opened the first crate to sample a few bananas – just to check they were of proper quality, of course.

We really did not intend to frighten the spiders into scurrying through the hospital windows. It just happened when we dropped the crate in our surprise. After that everything became very noisy and we thought it would be best if we came home…

Of course we had heard stories of big, hairy spiders hiding inside crates of fruit, but we really didn't expect that we would ever meet one!

Since getting home we have been listening rather anxiously to the local radio news and have just heard a radio presenter talking with a man from the zoo. We were most alarmed to hear him say that some of the spiders are tarantulas.

We do hope that the people from the Zoo manage to capture the spiders soon. The hospital staff and patients who were being interviewed by the radio presenter seemed ever so grumpy about having to stay outside in the car park.

Lots of love, Marigold

PS The bananas that we sampled before the spiders emerged were quite delicious! It is such a tragedy that they have all been confiscated.

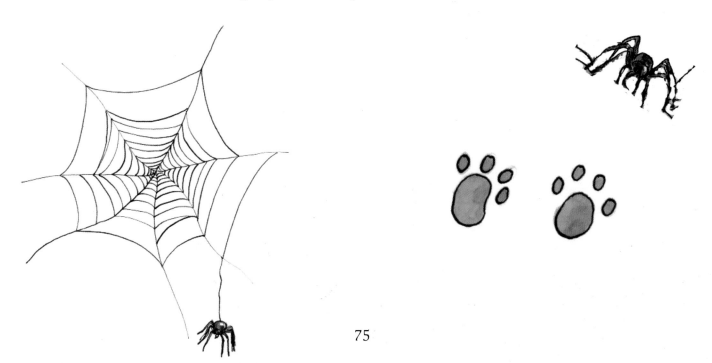

TREETOP COTTAGE
FOREST OF DEAN

Monday 30th April

Dear Granny Millicent,

Thank you for your letter. We were very worried when we read that Myrtle had trodden on a poisonous spider while you were all out for a day of hiking in Belize. Was it a tarantula? We do hope that she will be out of hospital soon.

I do wish that I could send better news but we too have had a rather difficult day.

You will recall that Montgomery has been training as a fire-fighter. We were so proud when he graduated last week and came home with his smart new uniform. So you can imagine our excitement when Montgomery telephoned

this morning to let us know that he, his fire engine and a large bag of best bananas, were on their way to the hospital.

After this, though, things seem to have gone a little wrong. There was actually quite a big fire at the hospital and Montgomery was set to work to squirt water onto the flames with the fire hose.

To be honest, I think the people at the hospital should be grateful to Montgomery. When I walked past on my way to the shops this afternoon I was most impressed by how sparklingly clean the hospital windows had become.

Montgomery, however, has been most upset to learn that some people are not pleased about the unintentional window-washing service. It seems that their office windows were open at the time…

The final straw for poor Montgomery is that he dropped the bag of bananas just as another fire engine arrived. He has just telephoned to say that he will be home late tonight. Apparently it takes rather a long time to thoroughly remove squashed banana from the tyres of a fire engine.

Ah well. We monkeys are always optimistic. And we have another, much better plan.

Loads of love, Marigold

TREETOP COTTAGE
FOREST OF DEAN

Wednesday 2nd May

Dear Granny Millicent,

We have been thinking very hard since the unfortunate incident with the fire engine and have come up with a marvellous alternative plan.

Montgomery is, understandably, not at all keen to return to our local hospital at the moment. Apparently all the people who were sitting close to open windows shouted at him quite horribly when he went to apologise to them. His paws were still shaking when he arrived home.

And so, at this evening's meeting of the English branch of The Banana Bunch, we decided that it would be wise to stay away from our local hospital for a while. But, as we cannot possibly abandon our banana delivery mission, we are now going to deliver our bananas to a different hospital in nearby Chepstow.

At first we considered travelling to the hospital by road but we are all a little reluctant to go anywhere near the Severn Bridge toll booths after Montgomery's distressing experience of imprisonment. And then Montmorency came up with the idea of travelling to Chepstow by boat. Sheer genius, and it will be such fun.

Sebastian is currently telephoning to organise the hire of a small boat while Montgomery studies some nautical maps.

I am a little concerned that no one in the family has yet worked out how to navigate using the antique sextant that we inherited from Great Great Uncle Magellan, but I am probably being unnecessarily anxious. The children are such clever monkeys that they are bound to work it out soon.

It is so cheering to know that, shortly after the people at the Chepstow hospital hear the splashing of oars, a large quantity of best bananas will soon be successfully delivered as they rest in their hospital beds. It is all so brilliant that I am going make a celebratory snack of banana flapjack with honey and banana ice cream to reward us all for coming up with such a foolproof idea.

Heaps of love, Marigold

TREETOP COTTAGE
FOREST OF DEAN

Thursday 3rd May

Dear Granny Millicent,

Oh my golly goodness! I was so confident that the journey to Chepstow would go smoothly. I could not have been more wrong. It has been a very difficult day…

I feel that I must make it clear that Minerva's sextant readings were not at all to blame for the fact that we found ourselves in the middle of the English Channel in the midst of a Force 9 gale. The lifeboat chaps who came to rescue us were actually rather impressed by how accurately Minerva was navigating our boat towards Chepsta in the Russian Federation.

We did feel foolish when we discovered our mistake but the chaps in the lifeboat were quite charming and could not have made us more welcome. In fact, they were so kind that we shared our last bunch of bananas with them.

Having reviewed the situation it has become clear that Montgomery read the wrong line in the index of the atlas.

Montgomery now has an appointment to see the family optician for an urgent eye test. And until that is sorted out we clearly cannot expect him to lead any further banana delivery missions.

I will be writing today to ask our family in Wales to once again take over banana delivery duty.

Lots of love, Marigold

PS The enclosed picture appeared in yesterday's edition of the *Lifeboat News*.

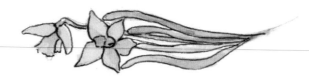

THE DAFFODIL HOUSE
SUGARLOAF MOUNTAIN

Monday 7th May

Dear Grandma Millicent,

Oh our goodness gracious. You did have a troublesome evening when you visited the Rodeo in Dallas.

It was jolly brave of you to try to ride the bucking bronco but we were most concerned to hear about your broken leg. We all have our paws crossed that you will be fit again in time for your canoeing trip in Canada.

As you probably know, the family in England have run into a few difficulties while trying to deliver their bananas. It is clearly time for the real experts to get back to work!

Bruiser and I have signed up for temporary work with a local cleaning agency. The outfits should make a perfect disguise.

Just as soon as we are sent to work at the local hospital we will take a large supply of highest quality bananas into the hospital, hidden amidst the mops and buckets.

I am sure that you will agree that this marvellous plan simply cannot fail.

Love and hugs from Magnolia

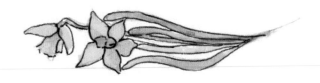

THE DAFFODIL HOUSE
SUGARLOAF MOUNTAIN

Thursday 10th May

Dear Grandma Millicent,

I am most awfully sorry to have to tell you that we encountered a small problem when we tried to deliver bananas while disguised as hospital cleaners.

It is such a shame. The disguise was quite brilliant and we very easily got inside the hospital, carrying a bucket which contained a huge bunch of best bananas, concealed beneath a duster. But then misfortune struck.

It all went wrong when Bruiser put the bucket down for a few moments so that he could run off to check that the coast was clear. When he returned,

ready to dash into one of the hospital wards to distribute the bananas, the bucket had disappeared.

We both searched frantically. When we finally located the bucket our hearts sank. One of our fellow workers was in the process of filling the bucket with hot, soapy water!

As you may imagine, we raced as fast as we could to rescue the bananas, but it was too late. They were already cooked.

It is all so disappointing. It had seemed such a good plan.

But never mind, the cooked bananas were not wasted. I used them to make a jolly good banana cake.

Better still. We have another plan.

Love and hugs from Magnolia

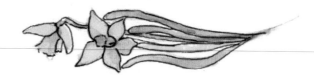

THE DAFFODIL HOUSE
SUGARLOAF MOUNTAIN

Monday 14th May

Dear Grandma Millicent,

Thank you so much for inviting us to join you next week for your mountaineering trip to the Rocky Mountains. After the events of the last few days, however, I am not sure that this would be such a good idea.

While he was at the hospital, working as a cleaner, Bruiser noticed that the building has lots of chimneys. And so a plan was born.

We decided that one of us would climb onto the roof of the hospital, and, while there, would carefully lower bunches of bananas down the chimneys into the wards. We really did think that it was one of our best ideas yet!

Yesterday afternoon we took a long ladder to the hospital. We were so proud as we watched Bruiser positively skipping up the rungs of the ladder onto the roof. Unfortunately he then looked downwards to wave at us...

I have to tell you that it came as a great surprise to all of us to discover that Bruiser is terrified of heights.

Needless to say Bruiser's yells attracted quite a lot of attention and there were soon people shouting and cameras flashing everywhere. It really was one of the most lively Sundays that we have had for ages.

Poor Bruiser still seems to be rather shaken by his experience and I have insisted that he must take it easy for a day or so.

Of course, he is reluctant to do so as he wishes to get back to banana delivering as soon as possible but I have put my paw down firmly.

I have packed the picnic hamper and we are going to spend tomorrow at the seaside. I am so much looking forward to having a quiet and peaceful day with Bruiser and the family.

Love and hugs from Magnolia

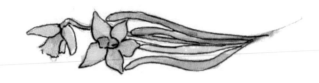

THE DAFFODIL HOUSE
SUGARLOAF MOUNTAIN

Tuesday 15th May

Dear Grandma Millicent,

So much for our planned tranquil picnic at the seaside! It has turned out to be a very vexing day.

Everything was going wonderfully until we dropped in to the local petrol station to get fuel for our car.

While there, Martyn (who is a wildly enthusiastic junior member of the lorry appreciation club) spotted a very smart lorry and could not resist going to have a look.

Once inside the cab of the lorry he was overjoyed to see a piece of paper that said "For delivery to hospital" sitting on the driver's seat. Martyn checked the address and, to his great delight, the lorry was en route to our local hospital.

It was too good an opportunity to miss. In an instant we had grabbed our bags of picnic bananas and had jumped into the back of the lorry.

We began to realise that something might be wrong when we had been on the road for over three hours.

When the driver stopped for a cup of tea we got out and made a most unfortunate discovery. The lorry had made the delivery to our local hospital earlier in the day and was now on the way back to the lorry depot in Stockport.

I am writing this as we sit at the roadside, trying to hitch-hike home. Thank heavens we have our picnic hamper and all those bags of good bananas to sustain us.

I will write again when we finally reach home.

With lots of love from a very dusty and footsore Magnolia

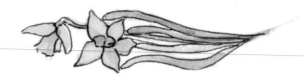

THE DAFFODIL HOUSE
SUGARLOAF MOUNTAIN

Friday 25th May

Dear Grandma Millicent,

I hardly know how to tell you the good news. Yesterday Murdoch and Mortimer delivered a positively enormous quantity of bananas to the hospital. They are so wonderful. I am bursting with pride.

For the last few weeks both Murdoch and Mortimer have been training to become postal delivery monkeys. Last Monday they received their uniforms.

Since then we have all been working frantically, with lots of string, sticky tape and brown paper, tying up parcel after parcel of highest quality bananas.

Yesterday morning our brave volunteers, cleverly disguised by their postal uniforms and red hats, delivered hundreds of packages of health-giving bananas to unwell people at the hospital.

Murdoch and Mortimer were overjoyed at their success and were happily chatting about returning to deliver more bananas today when disaster struck.

Just as they were entering the final ward Mortimer's hat fell off. Suddenly everyone was making a huge fuss about monkeys being inside the hospital again.

Mortimer and Murdoch had to run away very fast indeed!

But never mind. We were so thrilled by the news of their success that, when they did finally reach home, we all raised celebratory glasses of extra special banana milkshake.

We do wish that you could have been here with us to share the excitement.

With lots of love from a very happy Magnolia and family

PS
It is so kind of you and Grandpa to invite us all to join you for the final week of your world tour. It has been a rather busy few weeks here and a rest would be lovely.

It will be such fun to meet up with Marigold and her family. Between us, we are absolutely guaranteed to come up with all sorts of brilliant new plans for banana delivery…

Long Live The Banana Bunch!

A Monkey Never Gives Up!

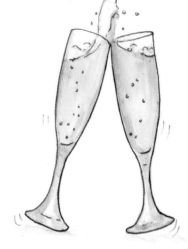

ACKNOWLEDGEMENTS

FOR ASSISTANCE GIVEN DURING CREATION OF
THE ORIGINAL PHOTOGRAPHIC CARDS

First and foremost – the author's father. When the author made the first card she assumed that it would be a "one-off". When a message came back from the hospital that Sheila was looking forward to receiving the next card the author gulped. And then her father said, "Well, I suppose the monkeys could parachute into the hospital with bananas." It was this simple sentence that inspired the entire sequence of stories.

The whole of the author's family – who came up with a huge number of potential story lines, helped with the fine tuning of each adventure and loaned clothing used in several of the photos.

Paul and Sue Shattock – for help with transport to and from Kingswood Fire Station to obtain photos for the "firefighter" stories and for providing a wonderful selection of plastic spiders for the "escaped spiders" story.

Christine Bush – for coming up with the story lines for several of the monkey adventures, encouragement and the loan of items for the "lifeboat" story.

Kristina Birch – for the loan of a motorbike and clothing used as disguises and assistance with creation of several photos.

White Watch at Kingswood Fire Station - for their kindness and cooperation during creation of photos for the "firefighter" stories.

Eddie Stobart Ltd – for allowing the author to visit their Cwmbran depot. Special thanks go to Ian Johnston (Newport) and Dennis Wood (Cwmbran) who so patiently hopped in and out of the lorry cab posing the monkeys for photos for Sheila's original "lorry" story.

Alistair McGowan, stonemason – who transported monkeys onto a high rooftop so that photos could be taken for the "bananas down the chimney" story.

Gwent Girl Guides who loaned Brownie Guide uniforms for the original "banana shortbread" story photos.

FOR ASSISTANCE GIVEN DURING PRODUCTION OF THIS BOOK

The author's family and friends – who have read and re-read draft versions of the text. Their encouragement and constructive criticism have been invaluable.

Linden Hare, the illustrator who has given so much of her time and talent to this project.

Aroon Ajmera – for advice on the pitfalls of publishing and self-publishing.

Jane Tatam of Amolibros – for superb professional advice and – just as importantly for an author and illustrator who are totally new to the publishing world – support, encouragement and humour.

Carolyn Bainton – for invaluable advice on content at the start of the project.

Robert McFee, pilot – who flew Grandpa Merlin into the UK to meet the illustrator.

John Hui – for his generous donation of computer memory sticks which made transfer of text between author, illustrator and publisher so much easier

Sharon Conner of monkeysgoneape.com.   A real treasure trove for monkey enthusiasts, and source of many items used in the original photos.

Judy Hindmarsh of The Bear Hotel, Crickhowell, for advice, support and introduction to Stephen Terry.

Stephen Terry for his whole-hearted enthusiasm and support for this project – not to mention the delicious banana recipe printed at the front of this book.

FOR RAISING THE FUNDS NEEDED FOR PUBLICATION OF THIS BOOK

Jo Grimes and Ezme Curtis who spent hours at car boot sales and online selling some of the author's personal clutter to raise funds for publication of this book.

FOR RAISING FUNDS FOR THE BANANA BUNCH CHARITY APPEAL

The very generous people of Abergavenny, Bath and Llanover who made marmalade, baked cakes, donated items and helped to make the first Banana Bunch fundraising day, in May 2012, such a success.

CHARITIES PERSONNEL

Natalie Barrington of Winston's Wish – who immediately grasped the nature of the project, bubbled with enthusiasm and offered much appreciated support

Elizabeth Waters – whose passion for the work of Tŷ Hafan, and enthusiasm for the stories and illustrations, convinced us to make Tŷ Hafan our second chosen charity.

TŶ HAFAN

Tŷ Hafan helps life-limited children, young people and their families by providing a much-needed source of strength, support and short break care for the whole family. Tŷ Hafan takes its support right into the family home and is there to help these families through every step of their journey. Tŷ Hafan is about making the most of the time available; allowing families to feel normal and do normal family things. It is about the simple stuff of life that you would want for your own family and your own child.

WINSTON'S WISH

Winston's Wish helps children rebuild their lives after the death of a parent or sibling, enabling them to face the future with confidence and hope. We are the largest provider of childhood bereavement services in the UK and offer the widest range of practical support and guidance to children, families, professionals and anyone concerned about a bereaved child. We know from experience that the right support, offered at the right time, can have a life-changing impact on bereaved children and young people.

Profits from sale of the first edition of The Banana Bunch will be paid into The Banana Bunch Charity Account, National Westminster Bank, Abergavenny, and will be distributed equally to the two charities by the account managers. At the discretion of the account managers a small portion of the profits from the sale of this book may be retained to fund publication of further editions of The Banana Bunch for the purpose of raising additional funds for charities.

Thank you for buying this book and helping us to raise funds for Tŷ Hafan and Winston's Wish.